LunaLu the Llamacorn

Written by **Michelle Lloyd**

Illustrated by Dee Driggers

Made in Charleston, SC
www.PalmettoPublishingGroup.com

LunaLu the Llamacorn

First Edition

Printed in the United States

Hardcover ISBN: 978-1-64111-989-4
Paperback ISBN: 978-1-64990-107-1
eBook ISBN: 9 978-1-64111-993-1

LunaLu the Llamacorn

Written by **Michelle Lloyd**

Illustrated by Dee Driggers

This book is dedicated to the
memory of my mother,

Marta Lloyd,

who was the greatest example of
true beauty shining from within.

LunaLu the llamacorn was a different kind of girl. She was a llama with a horn that made her famous in her little world. Everyone wondered how she got blessed with that golden horn, to which her parents replied, "The fairies gave it to her when she was born!"

They wanted a sidekick, a beautiful beast, to bestow a gift upon for her parent's good deeds. This special llama family kept them safe from harm when others tried to capture them and take away these good luck charms.

The fairies blessed
LunaLu with long life,
sweetness, and a golden
horn that would brighten
the lives of people, and
everyone would adore!

As LunaLu grew,
her horn did too, and
shortly people tried to
capture her to display
her at the zoo.

Although the fairies and her family worked hard to keep LunaLu from harm, some people captured her and took her away to a place where she didn't want to stay. The animals were in cages and displays that looked to be very strange. As LunaLu was placed in her enclosure, the animals around began to stare at her.

"So what are you?" the lions asked, and "Where did you come from with that big ole headdress?" "I am LunaLu the llamacorn from a place far away. I was captured by your people, and I guess I'll have to stay."

"Allamacorn?" the flamingos chirped, "That's stupid! There's no such thing on Earth!" "Yes it's true! I got my horn from fairy friends who live there too." "Well that's ridiculous, you look so silly! You should be on display at the circus with the clowns and their ringleader named Billy!"

"That's not nice, you don't have to be mean,
I am proud of my look and am not ashamed to
be seen!" The animals laughed and poked fun,
but LunaLu the llamacorn just ignored them
and decided not to run. Instead she listened to
visitors boast about her beauty, while the other
animals weren't given much attention really.

Soon the animals started to confess, "LunaLu we didn't mean to cause you distress. Everyone already loves you, and your stay has been short. We've been here longer and haven't had quite as much attention of this sort."

Animals across the zoo confessed,
"They think you're unique, one of a
kind, and love to admire you.
Are they out of their minds?"

"No, they're not," said the lions. "They see her beauty shine from the inside. What we thought was different is obviously good because everyone loves her like we all should. Even though we don't look alike, we aren't all the same. Being different makes us special, and that's where we get our fame!"

Eventually her parents and the fairies found LunaLu, and they decided to live with her at the zoo. The zookeepers decided to spruce up her home to match the attention she was getting from the beauty she bestowed.

Now all of the animals are the best of friends, and they all see that their beauty shines from within!

May you find your golden horn
for all to adore!

About the Author

Michelle Lloyd is a small-town girl and Elementary School Teacher from Lamar, South Carolina. Her biggest loves are her family and fur babies. Michelle has always enjoyed writing to display her colorful imagination. It has been her dream to write a children's book and looks forward to more adventures with LunaLu.

About the Illustrator

Dee Driggers is an Elementary Art Teacher who loves her students. She is thrilled for the opportunity to reach more children through illustrating LunaLu the Llamacorn and many more books in the future!

CPSIA information can be obtained
at www.ICGtesting.com
Printed in the USA
LVHW072328220920
666819LV00033B/1022